Translated by Elisa Amado

GROUNDWOOD BOOKS
HOUSE OF ANANSI PRESS
TORONTO   BERKELEY

THERE IS BEFORE THERE IS ANYTHING THERE

A SCARY STORY

BY LINIERS

And they turn out the *light*.

Then something incredible happens. Where there was a ceiling, now there is nothing. He could see the ceiling with his very own eyes. Now there's only a black hole... black and infinite.

He knows that they are coming. They come every night when the ceiling disappears.

It stands on the end of the bed without making a single sound.

It stares at him. It doesn't stop staring. It never says...

...anything.

And then more come down. Lots more.

He starts to feel scared because he knows what is coming next.

It comes every night when the ceiling disappears.

It is dark and shapeless.
Blacker than blackest darkness.

And it is the only one that speaks.
In a very low voice,
a whisper, it says...

He jumps
out of
bed.

He runs
out the
door,

down
the hall...

...to his parents' room.
His father says,

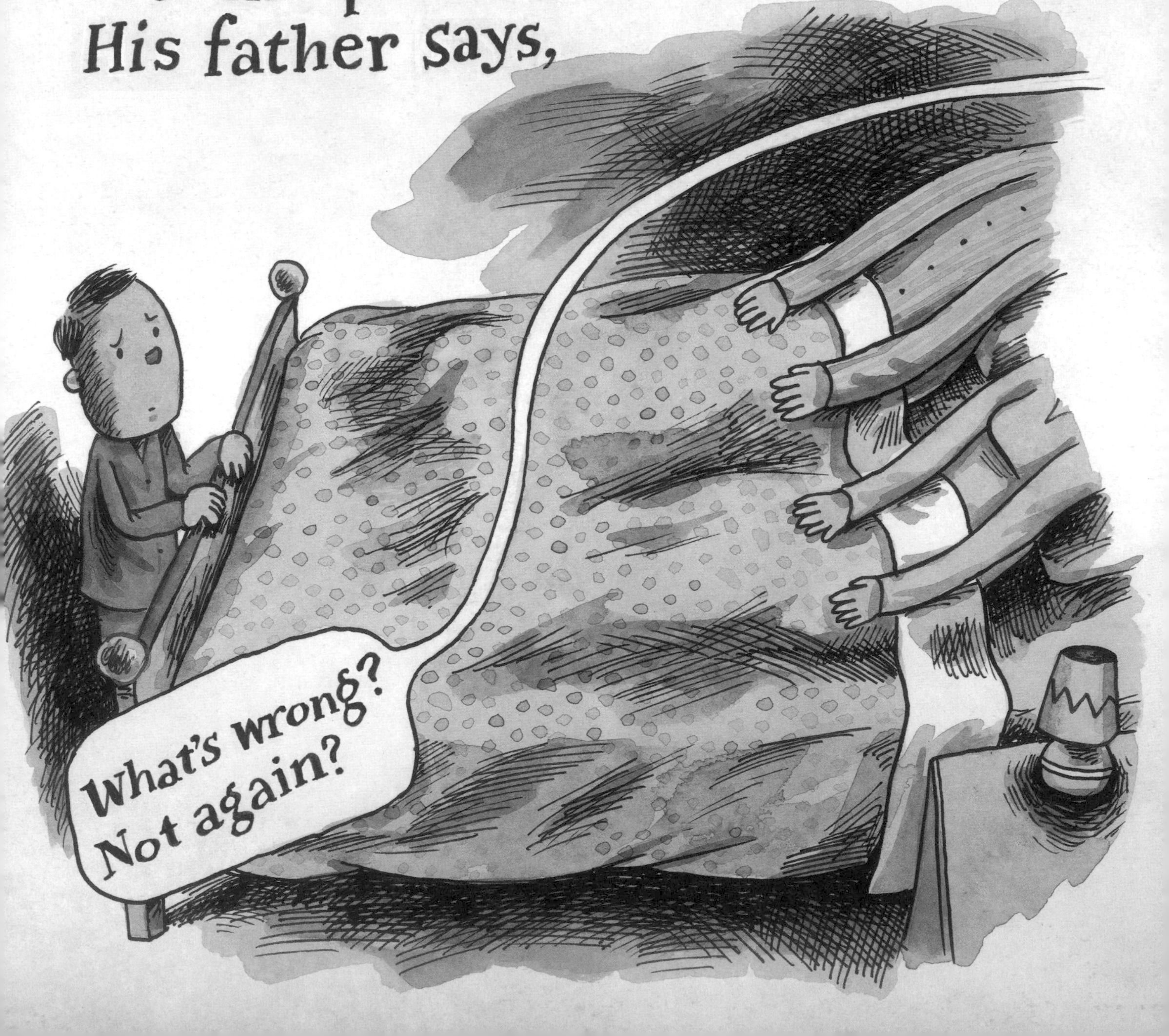

Dedicated to my parents, who turned out
my light and lit up my imagination.

Lo que hay antes de que haya algo by Liniers
Original edition © 2006 by Pequeño Editor, Buenos Aires, Argentina
www.pequenoeditor.com
Text and illustrations copyright © 2006 by Liniers
English translation copyright © 2014 by Elisa Amado
First published in English in Canada and the USA in 2014 by Groundwood Books

Groundwood Books / House of Anansi Press
110 Spadina Avenue, Suite 801, Toronto, Ontario M5V 2K4
or c/o Publishers Group West
1700 Fourth Street, Berkeley, CA 94710

We acknowledge for their financial support of our publishing program
the Government of Canada through the Canada Book Fund (CBF).

Library and Archives Canada Cataloguing in Publication
Liniers
[Lo que hay antes de que haya algo. English]
What there is before there is anything there / written and
illustrated by Liniers ; translated by Elisa Amado.
Translation of: Lo que hay antes de que haya algo.
ISBN 978-1-55498-385-8 (bound)
I. Amado, Elisa, translator II. Title. III. Title: Lo que hay
antes de que haya algo. English
PZ7.L6628Wh 2014   j863'.7   C2014-900941-0

Printed and bound in Malaysia